*For Mary Briggs*
M.W.

*For Edwina*
P.B.

Fun-to-Read Picture Books have been
grouped into three approximate readability
levels by Bernice and Cliff Moon. Yellow
books are suitable for beginners; red books
for readers acquiring first fluency; blue
books for more advanced readers.

This book has been assessed as Stage 10
according to *Individualised Reading*, by
Bernice and Cliff Moon, published by
The Centre for the Teaching of Reading,
University of Reading
School of Education.

First published 1986 by
Walker Books Ltd
184-192 Drummond Street
London NW1 3HP

Text © 1986 Martin Waddell
Illustrations © 1986 Patrick Benson

Reprinted 1987
Printed and bound by
L.E.G.O., Vicenza, Italy

British Library Cataloguing in Publication Data
Waddell, Martin
The tough princess.—(Fun-to-read picture books)
1. Readers—1950-
I. Title   II. Benson, Patrick   III. Series
428.6     PE1119

ISBN 0-7445-0540-2

# THE TOUGH PRINCESS

written by
## Martin Waddell

illustrated by
## Patrick Benson

WALKER BOOKS
LONDON

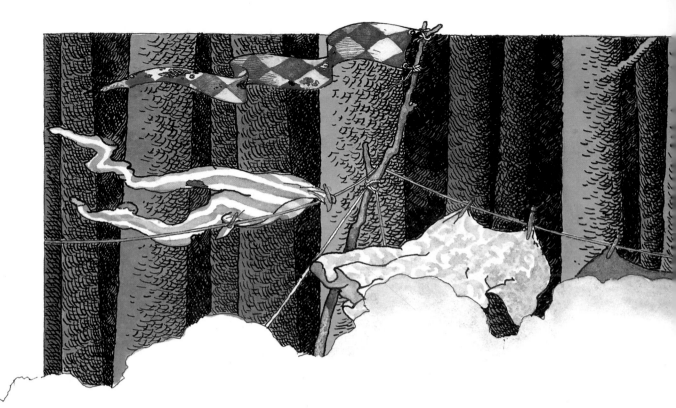

$O$nce upon a time there lived a King and
a Queen who weren't very good at it.
They kept losing wars and mucking things up.
They ended up living in a caravan
parked beside a deep dark wood.
The King is the one with the frying pan.
The Queen is the one with the hammer,
trying to fix the roof.

One day the Queen told the King
that she was going to have a baby.
'Have a boy!' commanded the King.
'He will grow up to be a hero,
marry a rich princess and
restore all of our fortunes!'
'Good idea!' said the Queen.
But when the baby came...

…it was a girl!

'Never mind,' said the King.

'She will grow up to be
a beautiful princess.
I will annoy a bad fairy and
get the Princess into bother, and then
a handsome prince will rescue her, and
we'll all go off and live in his castle!'

'Good thinking!' said the Queen.

'We'll call her Rosamund.'

'Ba!' said Rosamund.

The Princess grew up and up and up and up,
until at last there wasn't room
in the caravan to hold her.
The King got her a tent and
pitched it outside.
'It's time you were married, Rosamund,'
the King told the Princess
on her seventeenth birthday.
'Yes, Dad,' said the Princess, 'but…'
'I'll go off and arrange it,' said the King.

The King went off into the deep dark wood
to annoy some bad fairies.
The first fairy the King met was no use.
She was a good one.
She didn't even get angry
when the King
called her names.

The second fairy was bad, but
she was only a beginner.
She turned the King into a frog
for making faces at her cat,
but the spell wore off.

The third fairy was **very** bad.

This is her.

The King was awfully rude to her.

'Aha!' cried the Bad Fairy.

'What do you love most in the world?'

'My daughter Rosamund!'
cried the King hopefully.
'I will cast a spell on her!'
cackled the Bad Fairy,
who wasn't very bright, and
she darted off to do it.
'Good-eee!' cried the King, because
his get-the-princess-a-rich-prince
plan was working.

The Bad Fairy came upon Princess Rosamund
picking buttercups in a glade.
'Aha!' she cried. 'I am the Bad Fairy,
come to cast a spell on you.

Seven years shall you lie
Till a prince comes riding by…'

**Biff!** went Princess Rosamund, and
she knocked the Bad Fairy out,
bent her false teeth and
bust up her glasses.

'You rotten, ungrateful thing, Rosamund!'
said the Queen, picking up the Bad Fairy.
'I'll catch my prince my own way!'
said Princess Rosamund.
The next day she borrowed the King's bike
and rode off to seek her prince.

Rosamund had a lot of adventures.
She slew dragons and great worms and
black knights. She rescued several princes
who were quite rich, but she didn't like them,
and so she threw them back.
She did all the things a heroine ought to do,
but she didn't catch her prince.

Princess Rosamund grew tired
of rescuing princes and killing dragons,
and her front wheel got buckled in a fight
with a hundred-headed thing.
In the end she set off
sadly for home,
carrying her bicycle.

'Hello, Mum. Hello, Dad. Hello, Bad Fairy,'
said Princess Rosamund when she got home.
'Where's your prince then?' said the King and
the Queen and the Bad Fairy,
who had moved in by this time.
'Haven't got one,' said Princess Rosamund.
'I'm not going to marry a ninny!'
'What about us!' cried the King and
the Queen and the Bad Fairy.
'What are we supposed to live on if you can't
come up with a prince?'
'That's your problem!' said Princess Rosamund.
'I'm not going to…'
and then she saw the sign.

THIS WAY TO THE
ENCHANTED
PRINCE

'I'm doing this for me!' said Rosamund firmly,
and she set off into the deep dark wood.
'You lot can look after yourselves!'
She bashed up several goblins and ghouls and
the odd fairy (including several good ones
by mistake), and finally she won through
to the Enchanted Castle.
On a flower-strewn bed in the castle
lay a beautiful prince.
Rosamund gave him a big smacky kiss.

The beautiful prince opened his eyes and
took a look at Princess Rosamund.
'Cor! What a liberty!' he cried, and
he biffed her one, right on her beautiful nose.
And Rosamund biffed him one right back!
It was love at first biff.
They biffed happily ever after.
The King and the Queen
lived happily
ever after too,
and the Bad Fairy
got even worse.